MISTY'S
story

by
Jane Clarke

RED FOX

BATTERSEA DOGS & CATS HOME: MISTY'S STORY
A RED FOX BOOK 978 1 849 41180 6

First published in Great Britain by Red Fox,
an imprint of Random House Children's Books
A Random House Group Company

This edition published 2010

1 3 5 7 9 10 8 6 4 2

The Random House Group Limited supports the Forest Stewardship Council (FSC), the leading international forest certification organization. All our titles that are printed on Greenpeace-approved FSC-certified paper carry the FSC logo. Our paper procurement policy can be found at www.rbooks.co.uk/environment.

Set in 13/20 Stone Informal

Red Fox Books are published by Random House Children's Books,
61–63 Uxbridge Road, London W5 5SA

www.**kids**at**randomhouse**.co.uk
www.**rbooks**.co.uk

Addresses for companies within The Random House Group Limited
can be found at: www.randomhouse.co.uk/offices.htm

THE RANDOM HOUSE GROUP Limited Reg. No. 954009

A CIP catalogue record for this book is available from the British Library.

Printed and bound in Great Britain by
CPI Bookmarque, Croydon, CR0 4TD

Turn to page 93 for lots of information on the Battersea Dogs & Cats Home, plus some cool activities!

Meet the stars of the Battersea Dogs & Cats Home series to date . . .

Bailey

Misty

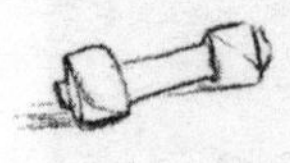

Chester

Rusty
Max
Daisy

A Big Change

Ruth Collins hurdled over the tree-branch jumps, raced along the wooden plank laid across two bricks, then threw herself full length on the muddy ground. She crawled commando-style under the tarpaulin that was held down with tent pegs.

"How fast was I?" she panted, pulling bits of twig out of her untidy hair. She was caked in mud and there was a

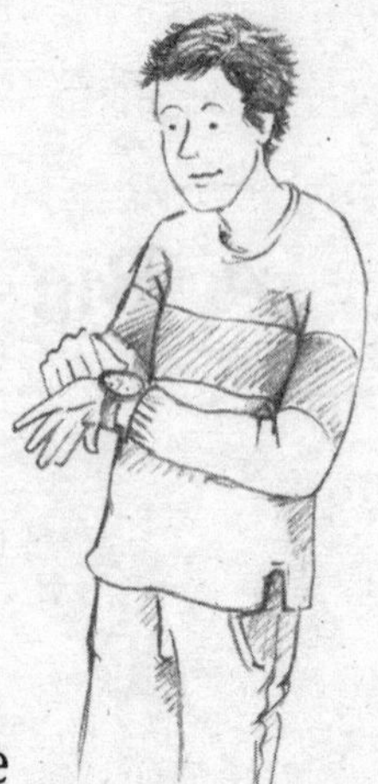

smudge on the end of her nose.

Her brother Ben pushed a button on his watch. "My stopwatch says forty-two seconds," he said. "That's three seconds faster than me. You won!"

"Yay!" Ruth punched the air in triumph. Then suddenly her face fell.

"You only let me win because you're off to university, and this is our last Assault Challenge," she said miserably.

"Cheer up, little sis." Ben rumpled her hair. "I'll be back at Christmas."

"But that's weeks and weeks away," Ruth sighed.

"Hurry up, Ben!" Dad's voice floated across the obstacle course they'd made in the back garden.

Ben put his arms around Ruth's shoulders as they walked to the car. It was piled high with Ben's stuff. Ruth could just see the end of his guitar, tennis racket and cricket bat peeking out from under a jumble of bedding.

"Time to go, son," Dad told him.

Mrs Collins hurried out of the front door waving a saucepan.

"You'll need this!" she said, shoving it in Ben's hands.

Ben popped it on his head.

"What is it?" he asked Ruth, with a fake puzzled look on his face. "A hat?"

Ruth smiled weakly at him.

"I'll really, really miss you," she said, trying not to cry as Ben stashed the saucepan in a box in the boot of the car.

"So will I!" Mum gave Ben a big hug, then stepped back. She took Ruth's hand and gave it a squeeze.

"Come and visit me when I've settled in," Ben said, getting in the passenger seat of the car. His face was shining with excitement. He wound down the window. "Give me plenty of warning so I can tidy my room!" he yelled as the car backed out of the drive. "Bye . . ."

"Bye, Ben! Good luck!" Ruth and Mum called, and, still holding hands, they waved wildly until the car was out of sight.

Silence fell around the house and garden. It started to drizzle.

"A new and fantastic part of Ben's life is just beginning," Mum said, trying to smile as she dabbed at her eyes with a tissue. "We should be happy for him."

"But it's so quiet now he's gone," Ruth sniffled, wiping away a tear as they went back in. "The house feels empty."

"It won't when we get—" Mum started to say, before stopping herself.

"Get what?" Ruth rubbed her face on the sleeve of her T-shirt. It came away muddy.

"When we . . . er . . . get Ben back home at Christmas," Mum said.

Ruth spent the rest of the day mooching around the house. It was hard to settle down to read a book or watch TV, or anything. Ben always played with her at the weekends – cool stuff like the assault course, and rounders, and tennis . . . And now he'd gone! Weekends will be really boring! Ruth thought, looking out of the window of her room.

The assault course is no fun on my own. If only my school friends lived in the same village, and not an hour's car-ride away . . . there's no one around here to play with . . .

"Dad's back!" Mum called at last. "Come down, Ruth. We've got something to tell you!"

"I don't want to hear about Ben's brilliant new life," Ruth muttered, stomping downstairs. Mum and Dad were sitting at the kitchen table. She frowned.

They were both grinning from ear to ear.

"What is there to smile about?" Ruth asked grumpily.

"A while ago, Mum and I decided something . . ." Dad said mysteriously. "We knew we'd all miss having Ben around when he went off to university—"

"So we thought now would be a good time to introduce a new member of the family!" Mum interrupted.

"What?" Ruth exploded. "Replace Ben?" She took another look at her mum and dad's smiling faces. "You're not having a baby, are you?" she asked in horror.

Mum and Dad guffawed with laughter.

"No!" Mum spluttered. "We thought we'd have a . . ." She was laughing so much she couldn't get her words out.

"A what?" Ruth was really confused now.

"A dog!" Dad said.

And that one word lit up Ruth's gloomy day like a ray of sunshine.

The Best Surprise in the Whole Wide World

"A dog!" Ruth gasped. "Really?"

"Really!" Mum said.

Ruth jumped to her feet. "A dog for me? One that I can play with?"

"Yes!" Dad laughed.

"We wanted it to be a surprise, to cheer you up after Ben left," Mum explained. "We agreed to wait until Dad got back so we could tell you together.

Only I nearly let the cat out of the bag earlier. Or should I say let the dog out of the bag?" She smiled.

Ruth giggled. "Getting a dog's the best surprise in the whole wide world!" she said. "What sort of dog is it?"

"You can help choose," Dad said.

Ruth clapped her hands and jumped up and down in delight.

"We'd like to get a dog from Battersea Dogs & Cats Home," Mum told her.

"I've heard of them," Ruth said excitedly. "They look after dogs who are unwanted or abandoned, don't they?"

"Right," Mum said. "They help find those dogs new owners."

"That's brilliant!" Ruth said. "When can we go and choose one?"

"It's not quite as simple as that," Dad told her.

"But we've filled in an on-line application form, and we've arranged to go to Battersea tomorrow and see if there's a dog there who will suit us. Sometimes that takes more than one trip."

"And even if we do find our perfect dog tomorrow, we won't be able to bring it home straight away," Mum warned. "Someone from the Home has to visit our house to make sure it's suitable."

"We've got a big garden, and lots of room to play. We'll find a dog that will love it here!" Ruth said happily. She thought for a moment. "Ben will love having a dog, too!" she said.

That night Ruth was too excited to fall asleep. What sort of dog will we get? she wondered. A big slobbery dog like a Labrador? A lean-machine greyhound? A pretty little spaniel . . . or a cheeky scruffy little terrier . . . or a gigantic Great Dane . . . or a tiny little Chihuahua I can fit in my school bag . . . or . . . or . . . Ruth fell asleep at last and her dreams were full of friendly woofing, waggling dogs of every sort, shape and size, and every one of them needed a home.

Ruth woke early next morning. For a moment, she lay in bed listening, trying to work out what was strange about the day. There were none of the normal disgusting boy noises coming from Ben's room! Ruth thought of Ben going off to uni and felt sad. He was a brilliant big brother, even if he was ten years older than her and had started going soppy about girlfriends . . . Then suddenly Ruth remembered.

We're going to Battersea Dogs & Cats Home today! She leaped out of bed, pulled on her clothes and dashed downstairs. Mum and Dad were already eating their toast and reading the newspaper.

Ruth glugged down a glass of orange juice, then grabbed a bowl of cornflakes and shovelled them down.

"Hurry up, pleeeeeeeeease!" she begged her parents as they sipped at their hot tea.

After what seemed like for ever they were all in the car and on their way. Ruth was so excited she wriggled around on the back seat, with a huge grin on her face.

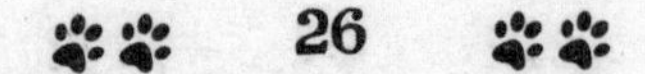

Finally they arrived. "Battersea Dogs & Cats Home!" Ruth read the sign by the green stairs at the side of the entrance. She raced up to the friendly man behind the reception desk. "We've come to choose our dog!" she said, hopping from foot to foot. She felt as if she was about to explode with excitement.

The Perfect Match

"We arranged an interview," Dad explained, joining Ruth at the front desk.

"Mr and Mrs Collins and daughter Ruth?" the friendly man asked. "We're expecting you." He led them to some comfortable chairs and they sat down. Ruth tried very hard not to wriggle.

"Your form says you have a big garden and can devote at least an hour a day to exercising a dog," the man said. "But you don't say what kind of dog you're looking for."

"Any sort!" Ruth leaped to her feet. "It doesn't matter as long as we love it and it loves us," she said, bouncing up and down impatiently.

"We'd like a dog with lots of energy," Mum told the man. "Like Ruth. Our daughter's used to hanging out with a very active elder brother," she explained. "But Ben's left home for university. Ruth needs the sort of dog she can play with. Preferably one that will wear her out!"

"I see!" The man smiled. "Come with me. We may have just the dog for you. She's worn out three dog handlers already!" he said with a twinkle in his eye. "I haven't dared to recommend her to anyone else, but you are just the kind

of family she needs. She's a bundle of friendly, boisterous fun."

"That's exactly the way I'd describe Ruth!" Dad chuckled as they followed the man to the kennels.

A sturdy little dog with a short white-and-tan coat bounded up to the bars, ears flopping and tail held high.

"Misty's a beagle," the man from the Home said as Misty wagged her white-tipped tail. "She can be a bit of a handful," he added, opening the kennel door.

"Misty!" Ruth flew into the kennel and threw her arms around the little dog's neck. Misty looked up at her with sparkling hazel-brown eyes. Then she wriggled out of Ruth's arms and tore round and round the kennel, weaving in between Dad's legs.

Mum raised her eyebrows. "Misty's certainly a lively one," she said as the little beagle stopped racing around and bounced up to them. Ruth got down on her hands and knees and bounced back at Misty.

A—ooof! Misty gave a strange low baying bark, and chased her white-tipped tail round and round. Ruth giggled.

"Beagles are great little dogs," the man said. "But they need to be part of an active family."

"That's me!" Ruth said.

"They take time and patience to train," the man went on. "And they don't like being left on their own."

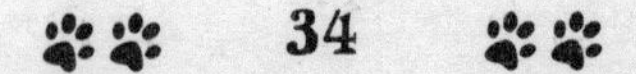

"Nor do I," Ruth said, scratching Misty behind her ears. Misty rolled onto her back so Ruth could tickle her pink tummy.

"If they get bored, beagles tend to chew things up," the man warned.

"At least you don't do that," Dad told Ruth.

"So we'd advise you to get a hard plastic bed, and metal bowls," the man went on. "And you'll have to beagle-proof your house and garden. They're very agile – they can jump up on work surfaces to steal food, and they'll jump fences and squeeze through gaps. Their noses come first – beagles are notorious for running off following scents."

Mum's mouth had dropped open. "Are you trying to put us off?" she asked.

"Misty's first owner couldn't cope with her," the man said seriously. "I want to be absolutely sure her new owners know what they are getting into. With proper training, Misty will make a wonderful companion, and I think you'd be a fantastic family for her. But I don't want you to assume it will be easy. It will be a challenge!"

"I'm happy to fence in the garden," Dad said. "What do you think?" he asked Mum and Ruth.

"I like a challenge!" Ruth said. "Pleeeease!" She looked pleadingly at her parents.

Mum nodded slowly. "Misty sounds like the perfect match for Ruth," she said.

The man from Battersea Dogs & Cats Home smiled. "That's great!" he exclaimed. "Sometime next week, we'll send someone to visit your home to check if it's suitable."

"I'll get busy on the garden," Dad promised.

"Meanwhile, Misty will have her health check," the man told them. "She's already been micro-chipped and spayed, and she's had all the necessary vaccinations, so that won't be a problem. If it all goes well, in a couple of weeks she'll be home with you!"

Ruth gave Misty a huge hug. "I can't wait!" she whispered into Misty's floppy ear. "We'll play and play! You'll love living with us!"

A New Challenge

"Welcome home, Misty!" cried Ruth. She leaped out of the car. They'd just collected Misty from Battersea Dogs & Cats Home and Ruth was impatient to show the little beagle around.

Misty flew out of the car and followed Ruth into the living room. For a moment, she stood in the doorway with her tail held high, the white tip quivering with excitement. Then *A-ooof!* she barked, and began to race round and round the settee. Two books fell off the coffee table as she skimmed past it.

"Take Misty outside to get rid of some of that energy," Mum told Ruth, handing her a little box of special doggy chocolate drops.

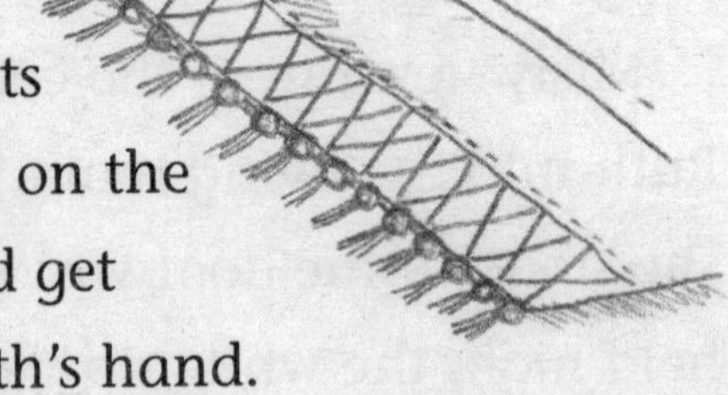

Misty spotted the treats and jumped up on the settee to try and get them out of Ruth's hand.

"Awww!" Ruth giggled as Misty's toffee-coloured ears flapped. The little beagle looked so cute bouncing up and down on the settee.

"Don't let her do that!" Mum said. "We need to make some rules around here."

"Down, Misty!" Ruth held a doggy choc low to the floor and the little beagle jumped down and gobbled up the treat. Ruth attached Misty's new lead to her collar and led her into the utility room.

"This is where you sleep," she said, picking Misty up and popping her into the plastic dog basket that she'd lined with a thick folded-up old towel. Misty jumped straight out again and stood by the back door.

"I don't like going to bed either . . . unless I'm really tired." Ruth smiled, opening the door.

Misty's tail wagged enthusiastically when she saw the garden. She put her nose down and began to snuffle around.

"Keep her off my flower bed," Mum called. "I'm entering my dahlias in the flower show at the village fair this weekend."

"OK!" Ruth said, pulling Misty past the flower bed which bordered the next-door neighbours' fence, and over to the assault course at the back of the garden.

"Sit!" she ordered. The little beagle looked up at Ruth and wagged her tail.

"Sit!" Ruth said again, pushing Misty's bottom down until she was sitting properly. "Good girl!" She unclipped Misty's lead and gave her a doggy drop.

"You have to learn how to do the assault course," Ruth told Misty, stuffing the box of treats into her pocket. "First we run and jump . . ."

Ruth took to her heels and hurdled over the three low jumps that Ben had made by laying dead tree branches on the ground. She rattled the box of doggy drops.

Ping, ping, ping! Misty hurtled across the jumps and sat, dribbling, at Ruth's feet.

"Good girl!" Ruth tickled Misty behind the ears as she gobbled down her treats. "Now for the balance beam."

Ruth ran along the wooden plank. Misty ignored the plank and ran along beside her, with her eyes on the box of treats.

"You have to walk along the plank," Ruth told her. She clipped Misty onto the lead and took her back to the start of the plank.

"Up!" Ruth commanded, lifting her hand into the air.

Misty jumped up – and over the plank. Ruth picked up the little beagle and plonked her on the wooden beam. Misty trotted carefully along it and jumped off the other end.

"Clever dog!" Ruth gave Misty another snack. "The tunnel's next!"

Ruth lifted up the edge of the tarpaulin and pulled Misty under it with her. Misty lay down beside her and licked her face. Ruth giggled. It was such fun commando-crawling through the tunnel with her dog! When they got out the other side, she gave Misty another doggy choc.

"You did really well, Misty," Ruth told her. "Clever, clever dog!"

Misty chased her tail round and round in delight, then sprinted off around the garden, sniffing at everything.

Ruth found one of Ben's old tennis balls.

"Fetch!" she said, throwing it towards Misty. Misty tore after it. Then Ruth tore after Misty to get it back.

"How did you get on?" Mum asked, when Ruth and Misty came in, both muddy and panting.

"It's fun having a dog!" Ruth said, taking an old towel and rubbing the mud off the little beagle. She was surprised how easily it came off Misty's short coat.

Misty dashed into the living room and leaped onto the settee.

"Down!" Ruth ordered. Misty jumped down. She put her nose to the ground and snuffled round the furniture. Then, suddenly, she shot out of the room and up the stairs as if she was following a scent.

"She's not allowed!" Mum called.

"Too late!" Ruth dashed after Misty. She was in Ben's room. Ben had taken all his posters with him, and his bedding, and the room looked bare and empty. All he'd left behind, propped up behind the door, was the body-board he surfed on when they went on holiday. Misty snuffled at it. Then she squeezed between it and the wall, and came out with something dangling from her jaws. She dashed past Ruth and scampered downstairs with it. Ruth raced after her.

The little beagle was curled up on the mat, chewing one of Ben's dirty, smelly socks. She looked at Ruth and wagged her tail.

"You can have it!" Ruth laughed. She took the new dog brush and began to brush the little beagle's silky-soft coat.

The phone rang. Mum went off to answer it.

"It's Ben!" she called. "He'd like a word with you."

Ruth reluctantly got to her feet and took the receiver. "I'll ring you back later," she told her big brother. "I'm busy grooming Misty!"

There was a hoot of laughter at the other end of the phone.

"It didn't take you long to stop missing me!" Ben said.

"I do still miss you," Ruth said guiltily, "but Misty's the most amazingly brilliant beagle. I'm teaching her to do the Assault Challenge."

"Cool!" Ben said. "You'll have to find a dog show for her to enter!"

Training Time

The next morning at breakfast, Ruth was slipping pieces of her toast underneath the table to Misty when she spotted an advert on the back of the newspaper that her dad was reading.

She could hardly believe her eyes. The advert was headed VILLAGE FAIR AND DOG SHOW!

"Let me see that!" Ruth grabbed the

Village News before her father even had time to object. She read the whole advert.

"There's a dog show at the village fair next Saturday!" she yelled, jumping to her feet.

Aoooof! Misty woofed.

"There are lots of different classes to enter . . . like the cutest puppy and the waggiest tail, and there's a doggy obstacle course," Ruth said excitedly. "That's got to be like the assault course! Misty can do that!"

At the sound of her name, Misty started racing round and round the table.

"Misty's having another mad moment," Ruth's mum groaned.

"Try to be calmer around her, Ruth."

"But we have to enter the dog show!" Ruth declared. "Misty can do it, I know she can!"

She sat down again. Misty stopped racing round, and looked up at her with shining eyes.

"The only other dogs around here are Bess, the farmer's old collie, the vicar's dachshund, Sausage, and Goldie the golden retriever and her puppy from down the road," she said, counting them off on her fingers. "Misty might even win a rosette!"

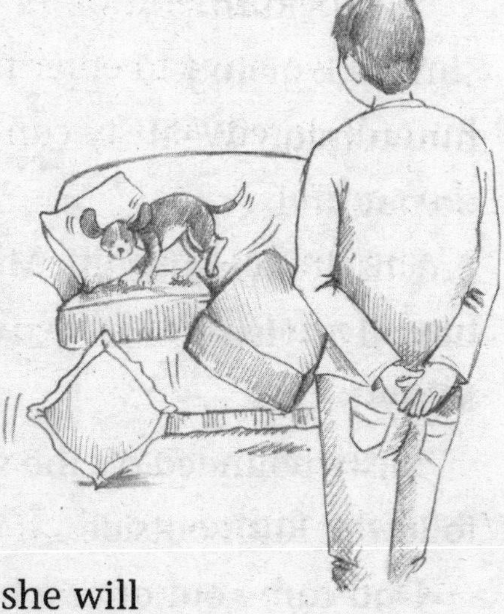

"She's not obedient enough," Dad said, watching Misty run into the living room and hurl herself onto the settee. "If she enters the show she will have to follow directions. The village fair's only a week away!"

"We'll work really, really hard," Ruth promised. "Pleeeease can we enter?" She looked at the advert again. "It says 'Register your name and the name of your dog in advance.'"

"OK!" Dad grinned. "I'll give them a call and find out a bit more about what you have to do on the day," he said.

"Yay!" Ruth shrieked, giving him a hug. "We'll go out and practise!" she said happily. "Here, Misty!"

Misty bounded off the settee and followed Ruth outside.

Dad came out after a bit.

"There will be jumps, a ramp leading up to a balance beam, a tunnel and a slalom," he told Ruth. "We've already got most of that set up!"

"What's a slalom?" Ruth asked, puzzled.

"A row of poles to weave in and out of," Dad explained.

"We can make one of those from bamboo sticks," Ruth said, running over to Dad's vegetable patch. She started to dismantle the bamboo wigwam that was holding up the runner beans.

"Whooooah!" Dad called out. "I'm entering those beans in the village fair!"

He went into his shed and brought out a bunch of bamboo canes. Ruth helped him push a row of seven canes into the soft earth in front of the jumps.

"Let's try them out!" Ruth got on her hands and knees and wriggled along, weaving in and out of the poles. Misty followed Ruth, her tail wagging so hard that it became a blur.

"She's getting the hang of that!" Dad said approvingly.

"Now, what can we use for a ramp leading up to the balance beam?" Ruth scratched her head. "Ben's body-board!" she exclaimed, and she raced up to Ben's room to fetch it. Misty followed her all the way up and back, and watched as Ruth laid it against the bricks so it formed a ramp up to the plank.

"Up!" Ruth ordered, gesturing with her hand.

Misty jumped straight onto the plank.

"She'll lose marks if her feet don't touch the board," Dad said.

"But the board might break if I walk up it to show her how to do it," Ruth said, taking a handful of doggy choc drops. She held them until they started to go gooey. Then she smeared a thick line of doggy choc up the middle of the board.

"That did the trick!" She grinned as Misty licked her way up the board and onto the plank. Ruth stood at the other end and held out her sticky hand. Misty raced along the plank, and licked her hand clean.

"If you two practise every day after school," Dad said with a smile, "I think you might do very well at the dog show!"

Mum joined them. "Just as long as Misty doesn't have one of her mad moments," she grinned.

Misty's Mad Moment

Monday, Tuesday, Wednesday and Thursday flew by. Ruth and Misty were up at dawn to practise on the obstacle course before Ruth went to school, and they carried on practising after school until it got dark. They got better and better and better at it, and by Thursday Misty didn't even need bribing with doggy chocs!

On Friday after school, Ruth burst into the house.

"The dog show's tomorrow!" she yelled. "It's our last practice! Come on, Misty!"

She opened the back door. Misty paused for a moment, sniffing the air. Then . . .

Aoooo! she bayed, and she set off with her nose to the ground.

"She's got a scent!" Ruth groaned as Misty zigzagged across the garden, her tail wagging enthusiastically.

"Here, Misty!" Ruth yelled. But the little beagle was deaf to her calls. She was heading towards the neighbour's fence. And just in front of the fence was a bed of big, bright and beautiful flowers.

"Misty! No!" Ruth shrieked. Too late. The little beagle dived into Mum's flower bed. Ruth was frozen to the spot in horror.

Aooo! Misty bayed, standing in the middle of the flower bed. Then she stuck her nose into the earth. *Tchoo!* Misty sneezed, and started to scrabble wildly at the ground with her front paws. Soil and dahlias sprayed everywhere as she kicked out with her hind legs. A muddy ball came flying out of the hole towards Ruth. Misty didn't even seem to notice. She was digging into the earth like a doggy bulldozer. Flower petals were flying around like confetti.

The muddy ball rolled to Ruth's feet. She picked it up. It was hard and shiny. So that's where Ben's cricket ball went, she thought. This will get Misty out of the flower bed!

"Fetch!" she yelled, flinging the ball as hard as possible in Misty's direction. The ball flew over the little beagle's head, and over the garden fence.

Uh-oh! Ruth thought.

There was a massive *crash!* followed by the unmistakable sound of tinkling glass.

Ruth's heart sank.

"What's going on?" Mum raced out of the house.

"My dahlias!" she shrieked in horror as she saw the devastated flower bed. In the middle of it, Misty was wagging her tail. Ruth grabbed her by the collar and dragged her towards the house. She was caked from nose to tail in mud.

"My window!" Another shriek of horror floated over the fence. It was Mrs Woods, the old lady who lived next door. "You'll have to pay for it to be fixed!" she shouted over the fence.

"Sorry, Mrs Woods!" Mum shouted back. "I'll be round in a minute to sort it out."

She glared at Ruth and Misty.

"That beagle is not under control," she said. "There's no way Misty can be let loose at a nice sedate village fair. Imagine the damage she could do!"

"But . . . but . . . the dog show . . . " Ruth spluttered, her eyes brimming with tears.

"Misty is not ready for it," Mum said sternly. "That's all there is to it. Maybe next year. But this year she will have to stay at home."

"It's not fair," Ruth cried, throwing her arms around Misty's neck. "It was me, not Misty!"

Aooo! Misty bayed mournfully. *Aooo!*

The Village Fair

The next morning was lovely and sunny, a perfect day for the village fair, but Ruth didn't want to go.

"I'll stay in the garden with Misty," she told her mum and dad, but they wouldn't let her. Misty howled as they set off to the fair without her. Mum was clutching a jam jar containing three beautiful pink dahlias she'd saved from the wreckage of her flower bed, and Dad had a plate of bright green runner beans. They headed for the village hall to put them on the country produce tables.

All the village had turned out for the fair. The first person to greet them was the vicar, with his dachshund, Sausage, trotting along beside him. Ruth wished she had Misty with her to say hello.

"Cheer up!" Dad told her as they headed onto the village green. "Have a go at welly-wanging. Ben won that last year, remember?"

"I'll never throw a welly as far as Ben," Ruth said miserably. She didn't know who she missed more – her brother or her dog. She mooched past the face-painting table.

"Would you like to have your face painted?" the girl behind the table called.

"Only if you can do a beagle," Ruth grumbled.

"I can!" The girl smiled.

Ruth sat down at the table. "My beagle has a black nose, and her muzzle's white with tan speckles and the rest of her face is tan . . ." she told the girl. "Her name's Misty, and I want to look just like her!"

"Misty sounds lovely," the girl said as she began to paint Ruth's face.

"You look just like a beagle," Mum laughed, when Ruth stood up. "Now you're in a better mood, how about some candyfloss?"

"Maybe later," Ruth said, admiring her reflection in the girl's mirror. "I don't want to lick off the face paint."

They walked on past the candyfloss and the hot-dog stall. Misty would love to sniff all these new smells, Ruth thought.

Mrs Woods was buying a hot dog. "Good morning!" she greeted them cheerfully. "You look just like that little beagle of yours." She smiled at Ruth.

"I'm really sorry about your window," Ruth told her. "I was playing with Misty and she had one of her mad moments,

and I was trying to get her attention and I threw a hard ball, which was stupid of me . . ." she gabbled. "But it wasn't Misty's fault, it was—"

"Don't worry, dear," Mrs Woods interrupted her. "The window has been fixed. Now, why didn't you bring Misty with you today?" she asked. "You could have entered the dog show!"

Ruth looked at Mum.

"I told Ruth that Misty couldn't come to the fair," Mum explained. "Misty's so boisterous and full of energy, she runs around all over the place . . . and Ruth can be the same way, too!"

"We were all full of energy once." Mrs Woods smiled. "I just wish I could still run around all over the place!"

Dad turned to Mum. "Mrs Woods is right," he said.

"Perhaps I was a bit hasty," Mum admitted.

"Then can I enter Misty in the dog show? Can I?" Ruth begged.

Mum and Dad looked at each other. "OK!" they said.

A strange electronic squeaking noise filled the air. The vicar was holding a microphone.

"This is a call for all dogs and their owners to assemble by the doggy obstacle course at the side of the hall," he announced.

"Quick!" Ruth gasped. "We need to get Misty! The dog show is about to begin!"

Top Dog

"First category: cutest puppy!" the vicar announced, taking out a red rosette. "This year's winner is Goldie's puppy!"

There was a round of applause and a lot of oohs and aahs as he gave the puppy the award.

Ruth rushed up with Misty. "We missed that one, but you're a tiny bit too old to win it, anyway," Ruth whispered in her ear.

"Waggiest tail, awarded by Mrs Woods!" the vicar announced.

Ruth and Misty took their place in the line. Mrs Woods went from dog to dog. Misty's tail and ears drooped guiltily when she saw her.

"Sausage is the winner of the waggiest tail!" Mrs Woods declared.

Everyone clapped as Sausage received his rosette.

The vicar took the microphone again. "The mayor will judge obedience," he said. "Tell your dogs to sit and stay, then walk away from them," he instructed the dog owners.

"Sit, Misty!" Ruth crossed her fingers.

The other dogs weren't doing very well. Sausage trotted after the vicar as if he was stuck to him, and Goldie ran back to her owner, who was holding her puppy. It was between Misty and Bess! But the farmer's old collie was fast asleep. Misty sat for a while, then began to wriggle.

She's getting bored, Ruth thought. Sure enough, Misty jumped up and gambolled back to Ruth. Will we ever win anything? Ruth wondered as the mayor pinned a rosette on the collar of the sleeping collie.

"And now," said the vicar. "It's time for the doggy obstacle course. Mrs Woods will be timekeeper. Oldest dogs first, please."

"That means we go last," Ruth whispered in Misty's ear. "Goldie's puppy is too young to take part!"

Misty watched with her head on one side as Bess methodically completed the course.

"A perfect round in forty-one seconds!" Mrs Woods declared.

The vicar looked at a list. "Sausage is next, then Goldie," he said. "Oh dear, I think Sausage is heading for the hot-dog stall!"

Everyone laughed as the dachshund skirted the first jump and ran off. Goldie wouldn't even start.

"She won't leave her puppy," her owner explained.

"And finally, Misty!" the vicar announced.

Ruth led Misty to the starting line and unclipped her lead. She hung onto Misty's collar. Misty couldn't wait to get started!

Mrs Woods took out the timer. "Ready, steady, go!" she said. Ruth released her grip on Misty's collar.

Misty set off like a flash of lightning.

She leaped over the jumps in super-quick time and wriggled through the slalom.

Ooooooh! The crowd gasped in admiration. Ruth thought she would burst with pride as the little beagle romped up the ramp and whizzed along the plank.

Then suddenly, at the entrance to the red polythene tunnel, Misty stopped and sniffed the air.

"Oh no!" Mum groaned. "She's picked up a scent!"

"Go, Misty, go!" Ruth yelled.

An eternity seemed to pass. Then the little beagle put her nose to the ground . . . dived through the tunnel and raced to the finishing line. She bounced up to Ruth,

wagging her tail.

"Good girl!" Ruth threw her arms around Misty's neck.

Mrs Woods was holding the stopwatch. "A clear round in thirty-six seconds!" she said. "Misty is the winner!"

"Hooray!" Ruth's mum and dad cheered as everyone clapped their hands. Misty chased her tail round and round in circles.

"The mayor will award a special prize to the winner," the vicar announced.

Ruth grabbed Misty and put her on the lead. Then the mayor shook Ruth's hand and presented her with a gold rosette – and a little gold cup full of doggy chocolate drops! Ruth beamed from ear to ear.

Ruth fixed the gold rosette to Misty's collar, and fed her a handful of treats. Then she picked her up and gave her an enormous hug.

A camera flashed. It was the cameraman from the *Village News*! He showed Ruth and her mum and dad the picture he had taken.

"You two look like twins," Mum chuckled. "We must send that picture to Ben!"

"Ben will think he has two doggy sisters!" Ruth giggled, looking at the two cute beagly faces in the picture. The face paint was rubbing off her nose. With Misty around, she thought, it won't seem long until Ben's home.

"Let's have some candyfloss to celebrate!" she said. She felt on top of the world, and it was all thanks to Misty, her wonderful new doggy best friend!

Read on for lots more . . .

🐾🐾🐾🐾

THE
DOGS HOM
BATTERSEA
PATRON -
ESTY THE QUEEN

Battersea Dogs & Cats Home

Battersea Dogs & Cats Home is a charity that aims never to turn away a dog or cat in need of our help. We reunite lost dogs and cats with their owners; when we can't do this, we care for them until new homes can be found for them; and we educate the public about responsible pet ownership. Every year the Home takes in around 12,000 dogs and cats. In addition to the site in south-west London, the Home also has two other centres based at Old Windsor, Berkshire, and Brands Hatch, Kent.

The original site in Holloway

History

The Temporary Home for Lost and Starving Dogs was originally opened in a stable yard in Holloway in 1860 by Mary Tealby after she found a starving puppy in the street. There was no one to look after him, so she took him home and nursed him back to health. She was so worried about the other dogs wandering the streets that she opened the Temporary Home for Lost and Starving Dogs. The Home was established to help to look after them all and find them new homes.

Sadly Mary Tealby died in 1865, aged sixty-four, and little more is known about her, but her good work was continued. In 1871 the Home moved to its present site in Battersea, and was renamed the Dogs' Home Battersea.

Some important dates for the Home:

1883 – Battersea start taking in cats.

1914 – 100 sledge dogs are housed at the Hackbridge site, in preparation for Ernest Shackleton's second Antarctic expedition.

1956 – Queen Elizabeth II becomes patron of the Home.

2004 – Red the Lurcher's night-time antics become world famous when he is caught on camera regularly escaping from his kennel and liberating his canine chums for midnight feasts.

2007 – The BBC broadcast *Animal Rescue Live* from the Home for three weeks from mid-July to early August.

Amy Watson

Amy Watson has been working at Battersea Dogs & Cats Home for six years and has been the Home's Education Officer for two and a half years. Amy's role means that she organizes all the school visits to the Home for children aged sixteen and under, and regularly visits schools around Battersea's three sites to teach children how to behave and stay safe around dogs and cats, and all about responsible dog and cat ownership. She also regularly features on the Battersea website – www.battersea.org.uk – giving tips and advice on how to train your dog or cat under the "Amy's Answers" section.

On most school visits Amy can take a dog with her, so she is normally accompanied by her beautiful ex-Battersea dog Hattie. Hattie has been living with Amy for just over a year and really enjoys meeting new children and helping Amy with her work.

The process for re-homing a dog or a cat

When a lost dog or cat arrives, Battersea's Lost Dogs & Cats Line works hard to try to find the animal's owners. If, after seven days, they have not been able to reunite them, the search for a new home can begin.

The Home works hard to find caring, permanent new homes for all the lost and unwanted dogs and cats.

Dogs and cats have their own characters and so staff at the Home will spend time getting to know every dog and cat. This helps decide the type of home the dog or cat needs.

There are five stages of the re-homing process at Battersea Dogs & Cats Home. Battersea's re-homing team wants to find you the perfect pet, sometimes this can take a while, so please be patient while we search for your new friend!

Have a look at our website: **http://www.battersea.org.uk/dogs/rehoming/index.html** for more details!

"Did you know?" questions about dogs and cats

- Puppies do not open their eyes until they are about two weeks old.

- According to *The Guinness Book of Records*, the smallest living dog is a long-haired Chihuahua called Danka Kordak from Slovakia, who is 13.8cm tall and 18.8cm long.

- Dalmatians, with all those cute black spots, are actually born white.

- The greyhound is the fastest dog on earth. They can reach speeds of up to 45 miles per hour.

- The first living creature sent into space was a female dog named Laika.

- Cats spend 15% of their day grooming themselves and a massive 70% of their day sleeping.

- Cats see six times better in the dark than we do.

- A cat's tail helps it to balance when it is on the move – especially when it is jumping.

- The cat, giraffe and camel are the only animals that walk by moving both their left feet, then both their right feet, when walking.

Dos and Don'ts of looking after dogs and cats

Dogs dos and don'ts

DO

- Be gentle and quiet around dogs at all times – treat them how you would like to be treated.
- Have respect for dogs.

DON'T

- Sneak up on a dog – you could scare them.
- Tease a dog – it's not fair.
- Stare at a dog – dogs can find this scary.
- Disturb a dog who is sleeping or eating.

- Assume a dog wants to play with you. Just like you, sometimes they may want to be left alone.
- Approach a dog who is without an owner as you won't know if the dog is friendly or not.

Cats dos and don'ts

DO

- Be gentle and quiet around cats at all times.
- Have respect for cats.
- Let a cat approach you in their own time.

DON'T

- Never stare at a cat as they can find this intimidating.

- Tease a cat – it's not fair.
- Disturb a sleeping or eating cat – they may not want attention or to play.
- Assume a cat will always want to play. Like you, sometimes they want to be left alone.

Here is a delicious recipe for you to follow.

Remember to ask an adult to help you.

Cheddar Cheese Dog Cookies

You will need:

227g grated Cheddar cheese
(use at room temperature)
114g margarine
1 egg
1 clove of garlic (crushed)
172g wholewheat flour
30g wheatgerm
1 teaspoon salt
30ml milk

Preheat the oven to 375°F/190°C/gas mark 5.

Cream the cheese and margarine together. When smooth, add the egg and garlic and mix well. Add the flour, wheatgerm and salt. Mix well until a dough forms.Add the milk and mix again.

Chill the mixture in the fridge for one hour.

Roll the dough onto a floured surface until it is about 4cm thick. Use cookie cutters to cut out shapes.

Bake on an ungreased baking tray for 15–18 minutes.

Cool to room temperature and store in an airtight container in the fridge.

Some fun pet-themed puzzles!

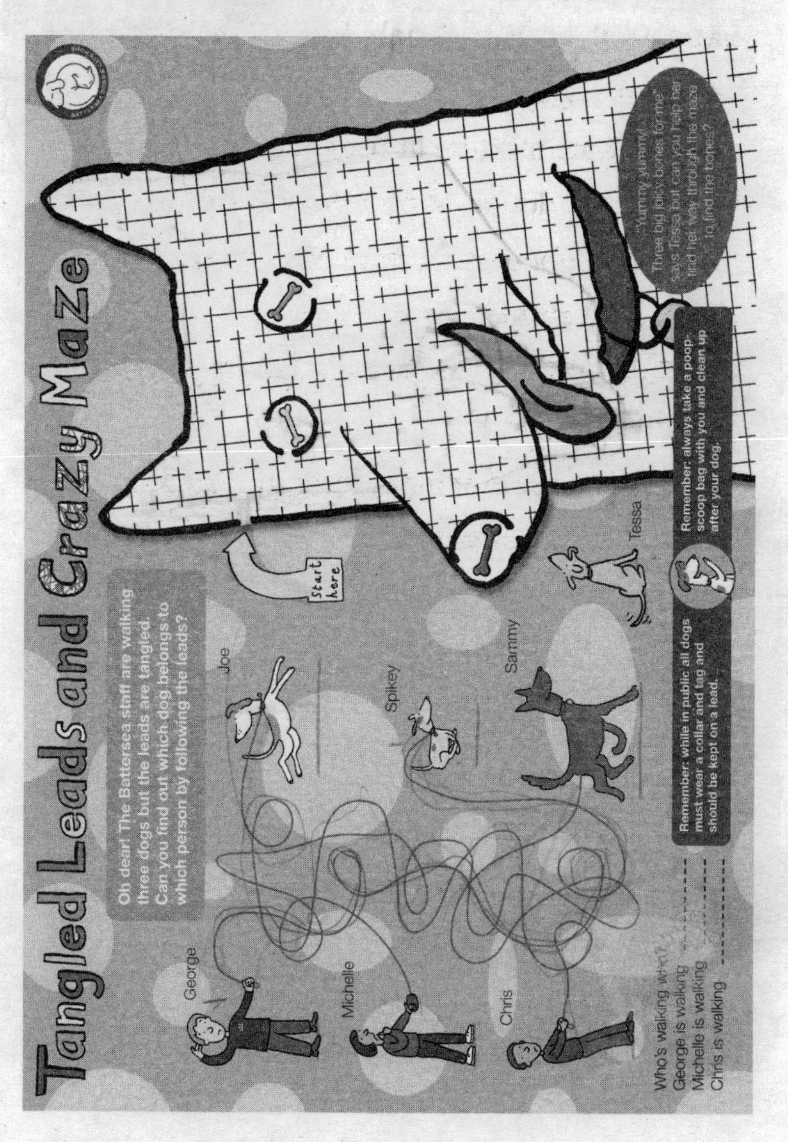

What to think about before getting a dog!

Here is a list of things that you need to think about before getting a dog. See if you can find them in the word search and while you look, think why they might be so important. Only look for words written in blue. They can be written backwards, diagonally, forwards, up and down so look carefully and GOOD LUCK!

SIZE
MALE OR FEMALE
AGE
COAT TYPE
COST
BEHAVIOUR
BASIC TRAINING
HOUSE TRAINING
TIME ALONE
GOOD WITH: PETS, CHILDREN, STRANGERS, DOGS
HOW: ENERGETIC, CUDDLY, STRONG WILLED, INDEPENDENT

I N D E P E N D E N T U N O P M S D H W
S X C V B N H R D G H I L J A N E V X Q
S F T I M E A L O N E N M K E R Q U S P
G T H S W V B J P X Z D F E H I Y J T M
A C V B O M G D F D S C T Y A A O P R W
F R O U Z C H I L D R E N C Y L I O A K
G D V B I D F J L Q W E V Z L C O Z N R
T G H Y J K L H M N F D S E R T J N G P
M U I L D F G O H K V M F E T Y J K E M
A G H D N C V U B C V P O G M T R I R O
L W X D Z V G S I Z E B F C E X P Z S I
E T Q U A D B E H D L N K Y A G E J G L
O R J C O A T T Y P E N B C X S T F H J
R J U J G D X R F H K U F D G Z S G O D
F O R X A O K A Q E N S N M Y I E Q Z L
E N E R G E T I C P A S V F H B N H X K
M W D F B V H N L K G R U O I V A H E B
A S Q E T R Y I D A C X B U K O Y T F C
L Q D S T R O N G W I L L E D N J M X Z
E H G V N H K G N I N I A R T C I S A B

Can you think of any other things? Write them in the spaces below.

Remember: when training a dog, reward works better than punishment.

Dog Breeds Crossword
Across
2 A breed used as police dogs and sometimes called an Alsatian. (6,8)
5 A dog that is a mixture of breeds. (7)
6 A breed commonly used as guide dogs for the blind. (8)
9 Smallest breed of dog. (9)
11 A brown/liver and white breed often referred to as sniffer dogs. (6,7)
14 A French breed with very curly hair, traditionally used as a gun dog. (6)
15 A small black and tan terrier that was used to catch rats. (6)
16 A small white terrier from Scotland. (6)
17 A small breed with short legs and a long back, sometimes called a sausage dog. (9)
18 The dog often used as the symbol of Great Britain. (7)
Down
1 A spotted dog from a Disney film that needs lots of walking as a pet. (9)
3 A breed associated with a brand of paint. (3,7,3)
4 This breed is used to herd sheep and needs lots of activity such as agility if kept as a pet. (6,6)
7 Eddie from the programme Frasier is one of these. (4,7)
8 A breed associated with a brand of shoes. (6,5)
10 Scooby Doo was one of these very large dogs. (9)
12 These dogs are used for racing but also make good pets. (9)
13 Smaller version of 'Lassie' dog. (7)
Help!
Ali's trying to count the dogs but some of them keep running about.
How many can you count?
Remember: all dogs need exercise in order to keep them fit and healthy and to give mental stimulation.

There are lots of fun things on the website, including an online quiz, e-cards, colouring sheets and recipes for making dog and cat treats.

www.battersea.org.uk